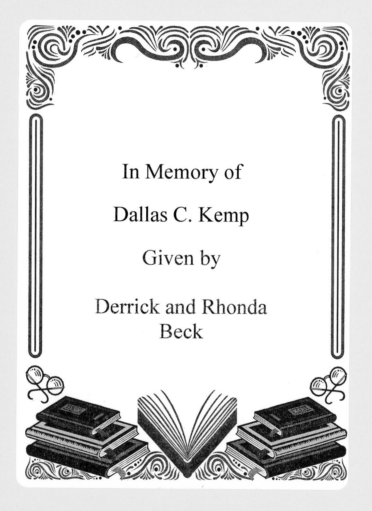

Over on the Farm

By Marianne Berkes

Illustrated by Cathy Morrison

Dawn Publications

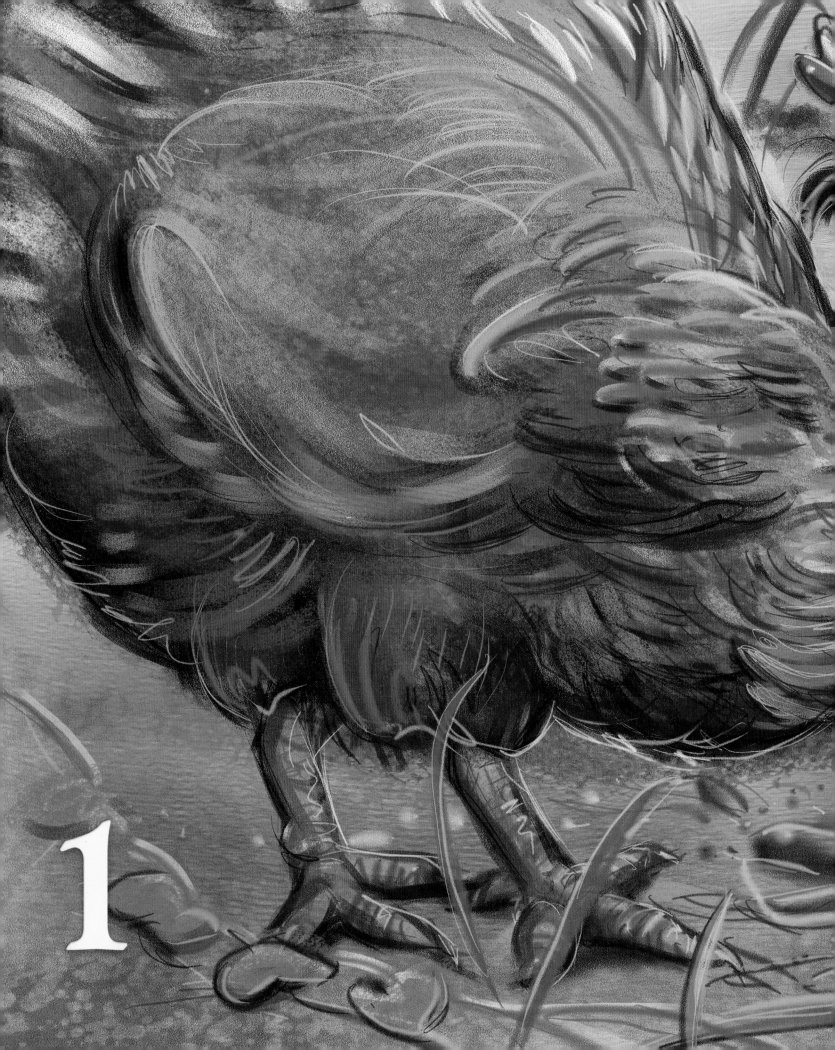

1

Over on the farm
In the early morning sun
Lived a busy mother hen
And her little chick one.

"Peck," said the mother.
"I peck," said the one.
So they pecked on the ground
In the early morning sun.

CHEEP   CHEEP

MAA

Over on the farm
Where they always have to chew
Lived a mother nanny goat
And her little kids two.

"Nibble," said the mother.
"We nibble," said the two.
So they nibbled on the grass
Where they always have to chew.

Over on the farm
Near a buzzing bumblebee
Lived a spotted mother cow
And her little calves three.

MOO

"Swish," said the mother.
"We swish," said the three.
So they swished with their tails
At the buzzing bumblebee.

3

Over on the farm
Waiting on the barn floor
Lived a clever mother cat
And her little kittens four.

"Wash," said the mother.
"We wash," said the four.
So they licked themselves clean
Waiting on the barn floor.

Over on the farm
Where the corn plants thrive
Lived a graceful mother horse
And her little foals five.

5

"Gallop," said the mother.
"We gallop," said the five.
So they galloped by a field
Where the corn plants thrive.

NEIGH

Over on the farm
Near a brood of little chicks
Lived a hungry mother mouse
And her little pups six.

"Hide," said the mother.
"We hide," said the six.
So they hid in the hay
Near a brood of little chicks.

SQUEAK

7

HOOT

Over on the farm
In a tree-hollow heaven
Lived a mother barn owl
And her little owlets seven.

HOOT

"Fly," said the mother.
"We fly," said the seven.
So they flew silently
From their tree-hollow heaven.

Over on the farm
Near an old barn gate
Lived a noisy mother turkey
And her little poults eight.

"Strut," said the mother.
"We strut," said the eight.
So they strutted in the straw
Near an old barn gate.

QUACK

Over on the farm
Where they followed in a line
Lived a white mother duck
And her little ducklings nine.

"Waddle," said the mother.
"We waddle," said the nine.
So they waddled to the water
Where they followed in a line.

9

Over on the farm
In a muddy pig pen
Lived a huge mother pig
And her little piglets ten.

OINK

"Roll," said the mother.
"We roll," said the ten.
So they rolled all around
In a muddy pig pen.

Over on the farm
Where the baby animals play
While their mothers all were resting
They up and got away!

"Find us," say the babies,
"From ten to one."
When you count them on this page
The story isn't done.

Go back on every page
And spy with your eyes—
Do you see the father rooster?
Isn't he a surprise!

Over on the Farm

Sung to the tune "Over in the Meadow"

Traditional Tune

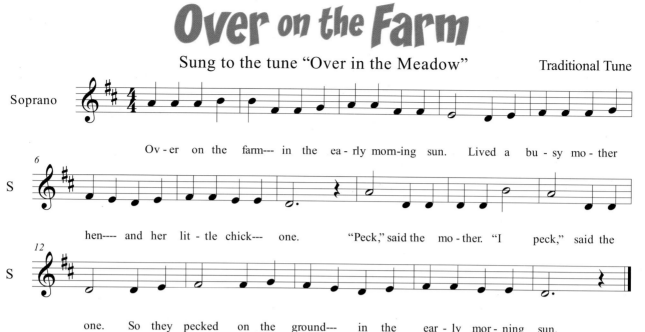

Ov-er on the farm--- in the ea-rly morn-ing sun. Lived a bu-sy mo-ther

hen---- and her lit-tle chick--- one. "Peck," said the mo-ther. "I peck," said the

one. So they pecked on the ground--- in the ear-ly mor-ning sun.

As you sing the story, invite the children to use different finger or body movements for each farm animal's action.

Chickens: Form a beak with your hand by putting your thumb under your other four fingers. Open and close your hand, as if you are pecking at something in a grabbing motion.

Goats: Pinch together your thumb and index finger and open and close while you move your hand back and forth to show nibbling.

Cows: Swing the fingers of your hand back and forth in the air to show a swishing motion.

Cats: Raise back of hand to mouth and pretend to lick.

Horses: Bend elbow and move arm in forward motion, alternating with other arm to show galloping motion. Or have kids stamp their feet in a galloping rhythm.

Mice: Cover your eyes with hands as if to "hide."

Owls: Spread out your arms and "fly."

Turkeys: Put hands under your armpits and move arms back and forth to "strut."

Ducks: With arms at your sides, spread out fingers and "waddle."

Pigs: "Roll" one hand over the other.

After singing the verse about the pigs, ask children to choose one animal and think of the sound it makes.
Then sing: *"Over on the farm, in the fields or in the hay, do you hear the animals calling? Can you tell me what they say?"*
Have everyone make their sounds at once to hear all of the animals on the farm. Conclude by reading
the rest of the story, giving children the opportunity to spot the rooster on each page.

FACT OR FICTION?

In this farm adaptation of "Over in the Meadow" by Olive A. Wadsworth, the animals really do peck, gallop, and waddle as they have been portrayed, but the number of babies they have is very different. That is fiction!

Here are the facts: Cows and horses usually have one baby and goats have two. Cats have litters of four to six kittens, while pigs often have ten piglets in a litter, and mice have even more. Hens raise as many as twelve chicks at one time. Barn owls usually have five to seven owlets in a clutch, and turkeys and ducks lay as many as eight to ten eggs.

Nature has very different ways of ensuring the survival of different species. Cows, goats, horses, cats, pigs and mice all nurse their babies after they are born, some for as long as two years. Ducklings and chicks bond with their mothers as soon as they hatch. In the case of the barn owl, both parents are fully involved in rearing their young.

SEASONS ON THE FARM

A farm is a place where fruits, vegetables, and grains are grown. Some animals are raised for milk, eggs, or meat. Activities on the farm change throughout the seasons.

SPRING

This is the time when most baby animals are born. As the sun warms the earth, new grass appears, and horses and cows are put out to pasture. Fields are fertilized and plowed. Seeds are spread and planted. Cows with babies produce milk, which is sold all throughout the year.

SUMMER

Vegetables and fruits grow and so do baby animals. Corn and hay grow tall, and the hay is raked and baled. Eggs are collected every day. As vegetables ripen, they're sold.

FALL

It's harvest time! The growing season has come to an end, and the last fruits and vegetables are gathered and sold. The silo is filled with corn or other grains that will feed the animals in the winter.

WINTER

The barn is made ready for animals to come inside where it is warmer. Inside, they are given hay and grain to eat. Chickens keep laying eggs and cows are still milked.

ABOUT THE ANIMALS

Baby **chickens** are called **chicks**. Hens are female chickens. A mother hen lays her eggs and sits on them for about three weeks to keep them warm until they hatch. She shows her chicks how to use their beaks to *peck* the ground to look for food in the barnyard.

Baby **goats** are called **kids**. Goats are almost always chewing. They like to *nibble* on grass. Their saliva makes food wet enough to swallow, and it goes into one part of the goat's stomach. When that part of the stomach is full, the goat brings up a wad of food and chews it again before it goes into another part of its stomach to be digested.

Baby **cows** are called **calves**. Cows spend a lot of time in fields where they eat grass. They often *swish* their tails when insects bother them. Like goats, cows have a special stomach that allows them to cough up a wad of grass or hay they've swallowed. This wad is called cud. They chew their cud a second time and swallow it again. When a cow has a baby she makes milk for her calf, and the extra milk is sold for people to drink.

Baby **cats** are called **kittens**. Cats like to keep themselves very clean, and kittens begin to *wash* themselves when they're about four weeks old. Sometimes they use their rough tongues to lick their fur. Other times they lick one paw to apply saliva. Then they wipe the paw over their face or body, like the way we might use a wash cloth.

Baby **horses** are called **foals**. Horses have a hard covering on each foot called a hoof. To help protect their hooves and make them last longer as they *gallop* or trot, people put U-shaped metal plates—horseshoes—onto the rims of a horse's hooves. For thousands of years, horses helped farmers plow fields and pull carts to markets.

Baby **mice** are called **pups**. Mice are rodents that can be found on farms worldwide. They often build nests in the hay and *hide* there away from cats, dogs, hawks, owls and other animals that would eat them. At night they scurry along the ground looking for grain, seeds, and other food to eat.

Baby **barn owls** are called **owlets**. Barn Owls live in holes in trees and sometimes in barn lofts and other human structures. They are active at night and rely on their very good hearing as they *fly* silently for a surprise attack on rats, mice, and voles. Farmers like them because they act as a natural pest control.

Baby **turkeys** are called **poults**. Turkeys are farm birds raised for their meat all year round, not just at Thanksgiving. During the mating season, the males (toms) *strut* to attract females by fanning out their tail feathers and dragging their wings along the ground. Sometimes poults seem to be strutting, too.

Baby **ducks** are called **ducklings**. Ducks are called waterfowl because they're often found at farm ponds or other bodies of water. The white Peking duck is a common farm duck. Their webbed feet act like paddles when swimming. But when walking on land, their webbed feet cause them to *waddle*. Ducklings follow their mother in a line.

Baby **pigs** are called **piglets**. Pigs have sensitive skin with very little hair to protect it. They *roll* in mud to cover their skin so it doesn't get sunburned. A pigpen may look messy, but it's really not. Pigs are actually quite clean. They even have a special corner in their pen for their "toilet."

Roosters have been on farms throughout history. A rooster, as shown in this story, is a male chicken. Roosters are famous for their early morning crowing (cock-a-doodle-do). But, in fact, they will crow at any time throughout the day. Farms usually have many hens, but just one rooster. He mates with most or all of the female hens (chickens) on the farm, ensuring an ongoing supply of fertile eggs. Hens can still lay eggs if there is no rooster, but the eggs will not hatch. A rooster often sits on a high lookout perch and serves as a guard, warning the hens when he senses danger. He also calls his hens when he has found a food source.

MORE FUN ON THE FARM

MATH

These two activities use plastic eggs. Twelve eggs is a good number to begin with for young children, but for older children you may want to use up to 20 eggs.

Subtraction: Place plastic eggs in a basket and appoint one child to be a "farmer." Give the basket to the "farmer" and have the farmer count the eggs and tell the class how many there are. The farmer takes out one or two eggs and asks the class how many are left. The first student who identifies the correct number becomes the farmer. The game continues with each new farmer taking out one, two, or three eggs until none are left.

Addition: Show the class plastic eggs in a box. Take out two eggs and place them in a basket. Appoint a child to be a "hen." Have the hen select one, two, or three eggs from the box and add them to the basket. The student who correctly identifies how many eggs are now in the basket becomes the next hen. The game continues until all of the eggs are out of the box and in the basket.

SCIENCE

Touch and Tell: Bring in various fruits and vegetables that are grown on a farm. Put them in a big pail and have children try to guess what they are by feeling them. No peeking!

Grow Your Own Bean: Dampen a sheet of paper towel with water, crumble it up, and put it in a clear plastic cup. Push a lima bean down the side of the cup and watch it grow. Young children will be fascinated to watch the roots shooting down and tiny leaves emerging. Make sure to keep the paper towel continuously moist.

Plants from a Carrot Top: Cut the top off a carrot (about 2 inches). Stick a toothpick into either side of the carrot stump and rest it on top of a small glass filled with water so that the bottom of the carrot stump is touching the water. Keep the water touching the edge of the stump. Explain to children that a carrot is a root and it will not grow more carrots, but it will grow pretty fern-like leaves—a carrot top.

Birds and Eggs: Ask children to name all of the birds in the story—hen (chicken), owl, turkey, and duck. Draw or cut out pictures of these birds' actual eggs. Have children compare the eggs by size, shape, and color. Include other eggs to compare, such as an ostrich egg (largest egg) or a hummingbird egg (smallest egg).

LANGUAGE ARTS

Rhyme and Repetition: Practice listening skills by reading a page and asking the children to listen for the word that rhymes with the number. For example: one/sun, two/chew, three/bee, four/floor, five/thrive, six/chicks, seven/heaven, eight/gate, nine/line, ten/den. Then ask them what words were repeated on every page.

Word and Number Matching: Write numerals 1 through 10 on index cards. On another set of index cards write the words "one" through "ten." Have children match the cards.

ART

Seasons: Fold a piece of 8x10 white paper into four quarters. Each section is a different season of the year: spring, summer, autumn and winter, in that order. Ask children to draw a picture of what would be happening on the farm during each season. Have them include different animals for each season.

Muddy Pigs: Cut out pig shapes from pink construction paper. Have children glue the pink pigs onto brown paper. Create "mud" by mixing a little brown paint into some shaving cream. Give each child a small cup of "mud" and a paint brush and have them cover their pigs in mud, or use brown markers or crayons instead of paint.

Farm Chores: Give children a white paper plate and have them draw two lines to create four quarters. In each quarter, have children draw what they think the farmer does every day. For example, collecting eggs, milking a cow, feeding the pigs, lassoing a horse, fixing the barn, riding a tractor, building a gate, sowing seeds, or plowing fields.

FROM FARM TO TABLE

Making Butter: Pour heavy cream in a jar and secure the lid very tightly. Then shake, shake, shake! You can make one container of butter using a large mason jar and pass it around so each child has a turn to shake. Or you can use baby food jars to give children their own individual container. In a large jar, it will take about 20 minutes for the milk to solidify. Baby food jars take about 10 minutes. Sing some farm songs while you shake. The process is complete when you have a fairly solid mass at the bottom of the jar. Pour off the buttermilk. If you like, stir in some kosher salt before spreading the butter on crackers.

Honey Corn: Children can also use their homemade butter with this downloadable recipe from *What's in the Garden?* also by Marianne Berkes. With an adult, remove husks and silk from 4 ears of corn. Fill a large pot half full with water and bring to a boil. Stir in 2 tbsp. of honey and then drop in the corn. Cook 3 to 4 minutes. Lift the corn out of the water with tongs and drain on paper towels. Serve with butter, salt, and pepper.

MOVEMENT AND MUSIC

Animals in the Barn: Put a big hoop down on the floor and tell the children it's a pretend barn. Ask a child to step into the " barn" and become one of the animals from the book. Explain that as they leave the barn (step out of the hoop) they will act out how the animal moves. Emphasize that they can use actions but no sounds. For example, the horse could gallop, the duck could waddle, the owl could fly, etc. Help children really think about how their animal moves by asking questions, such as, "Does the animal walk on all fours?" "Does it use its tail?" Have the rest of the class guess what animal is being acted out. The child who guesses correctly is the next person in the "barn."

Stand Up, Sit Down: Give each child a bookmark (available on the Dawn Publications website). Make sure children can identify the baby animal on their bookmark. Have them follow your directions to stand up or sit down. For example, say:

1. Chicks stand up.
2. Calves and kittens stand up.
3. Foals stand up.
4. Chicks and kittens sit down.
5. Piglets stand up.
6. Foals sit down. (Continue using all of the baby animals.)

You can also do this activity with the types of fruits and vegetables grown on the farm. Use colored construction paper and have children draw and cut out common foods, such as corn (yellow), pumpkins (orange), beans (green), apples (red), etc. Tape the cutouts to straws or tongue depressors and play as you did with the baby animals.

Adapt a Song: Sing about farm animal babies using the tune to "The Wheels on the Bus." In each verse include the name of the baby, the sound it makes, and where the babies are in this story. For example:

The chicks on the ground go cheep cheep cheep,

Cheep, cheep, cheep.

Cheep, cheep, cheep.

The chicks on the ground go cheep, cheep, cheep

All around the farm.

The kids in the grass go maa, maa, maa.

The calves in the pasture go moo, moo, moo.

The kittens on the floor go mew, mew, mew

The foals in the field go neigh, neigh, neigh.

And so on.

Teachers and Parents: There are additional resources online, including engaging lesson plans, easy-to-do activities, and free downloadable bookmarks of each of the baby farm animals. Go to www.dawnpub.com and click on "Activities," or scan this code.

Marianne Berkes spent much of her life as an early childhood educator, children's theater director, and children's librarian. She is the award-winning author of over 20 "interactive" picture books that make learning fun. Her books, inspired by her love of nature, open kids' eyes to the magic found in our natural world. Ever since she wrote *Over in the Ocean*, teachers and students have suggested she write *Over on the Farm*. But she was busy researching for her other "Over" habitat books, including Rainforest, Arctic, Australia, Forest, River, Mountain, and finally, Grasslands (due out in Fall, 2016). Now that her "Over" habitat books are complete, *Over on the Farm* has become a reality. Marianne hopes young children will want to read it again and again, each time learning something new and exciting. Her web site is www.MarianneBerkes.com.

Cathy Morrison is an award-winning illustrator in Colorado who grew up spending most summers on her family farm in Texas. The farm included many cows, two horses, several pigs, no chickens, but there was one peacock. She began her career in animation and graphic design, but discovered her passion for children's book illustration while raising her two children. After several years illustrating with traditional media, she now works digitally, which helps the publisher adapt the art into interactive book apps. This is Cathy's fourth book for Dawn Publications.

To the Vanderslice family with love from Mama M. And for Sandy and her chickens. — MB

To a girl named Owen. — CM

Library of Congress Cataloging-in-Publication Data
Over on the farm / by Marianne Berkes ; illustrated by Cathy Morrison. -- First edition.
    pages cm
  Summary: A counting book in rhyme presents various farm animals and their offspring, from a mother hen and her "little chick one" to a mother pig and her "little piglets ten." Includes related facts and activities.
  Includes bibliographical references.
  ISBN 978-1-58469-548-6 (hardback) -- ISBN 978-1-58469-549-3 (pbk.) [1. Stories in rhyme. 2. Domestic animals--Fiction. 3. Animals--Infancy--Fiction. 4. Counting.] I. Morrison, Cathy, illustrator. II. Title.

PZ8.3.B4557Owr 2016
[E]--dc23
                    2015014711

Book design and computer production by Patty Arnold, *Menagerie Design & Publishing*

Manufactured by Regent Publishing Services, Hong Kong
Printed December, 2015, in ShenZhen, Guangdong, China

10 9 8 7 6 5 4 3 2 1
First Edition

ALSO BY MARIANNE BERKES

Over in the Ocean: In a Coral Reef — With unique and outstanding style, this book portrays a vivid community of marine creatures.

Over in the Jungle: A Rainforest Rhyme — As with *Ocean*, this book captures a rain forest teeming with remarkable animals.

Over in the Forest: Come and Take a Peek — Follow the tracks of forest animals, but watch out for the skunk!

Over in the Arctic: Where the Cold Winds Blow — Another charming counting rhyme introduces creatures of the tundra.

Over in a River: Flowing Out to the Sea — Beavers, manatees and so many more animals help teach the geography of 10 great North American rivers.

Over in Australia: Amazing Animals Down Under — Australian animals are often unique, many with pouches for the babies. Such fun!

Over on a Mountain: Somewhere in the World — Twenty cool animals, ten great mountain ranges, and seven continents all in one story!

Going Around the Sun: Some Planetary Fun — Earth is part of a fascinating "family" of planets. Here's a glimpse of the "neighborhood."

Going Home: The Mystery of Animal Migration — Many animals migrate "home," often over great distances. A solid introduction to the phenomenon of migration.

Seashells by the Seashore — Kids discover, identify, and count twelve beautiful shells to give Grandma for her birthday.

The Swamp Where Gator Hides — Still as a log, only his watchful eyes can be seen. But when gator moves, he really moves!

What's in the Garden? — Good food doesn't begin on a store shelf in a box. It comes from a garden bursting with life!

MAY WE ALSO RECOMMEND . . .

Molly's Organic Farm is based on the true story of homeless cat that found herself in the wondrous world of an organic farm—seen through Molly's eyes.

Green Bean! Green Bean! — A freckled-faced young gardener opens a packet of seeds and the magic begins! She harvests a full season of fun and experience.

Mighty Mole and Super Soil — Below your feet, Mighty Mole is on the move, like a swimmer in dirt. Her largely invisible ecosystem is vital to the health of the world.

The Prairie That Nature Built — A romp above, below, and all around a beautiful and exciting habitat. There's nothing boring about a prairie!

Pitter and Patter — Take a ride with Pitter on a water cycle! You'll go through a watershed, down, around and up again. Oh, the places you'll go . . .

In the Trees, Honeybees! — Get an inside-the-hive view of a wild colony of honey bees. Simple verse will engage a young child, with fascinating facts to satisfy an older child.

The Mouse and the Meadow — A curious young mouse boldly ventures into the meadow for the first time. There he gets a crash course about life from creatures both friendly and not so friendly.

Dandelion Seed's Big Dream — A charming tale that follows a seed as it floats from the countryside to the city and encounters all sorts of obstacles and opportunities.

On Kiki's Reef — Swim with Kiki, a baby sea turtle, as she grows to become a gentle giant and discovers life on a busy coral reef...lots of surprises!

Jo MacDonald Had a Garden. E-I-E-I-O! Young Jo, granddaughter of Old MacDonald, discovers the delights of a garden—and also the pond and woods on the farm, in **Jo MacDonald Saw a Pond** and **Jo MacDonald Hiked in the Woods**.

Dawn Publications is dedicated to inspiring in children a deeper understanding and appreciation for all life on Earth. You can browse through our titles, download resources for teachers, and order at www.dawnpub.com or call 800-545-7475.